The Three Billy Goats Gruff

Barrie Wade and Nicola Evans

W

Once upon a time there were three Billy Goats Gruff.

They lived happily in their field, until they ate all the grass. Then the three Billy Goats Gruff were very hungry.

4

They looked longingly across the river bridge. Sweet grass grew in the lush meadow on the other side of the river...

…but a wicked old troll lived under the bridge and he was hungry too. He had often wished the three Billy Goats Gruff would come out of their field.

"I am so hungry!" the littlest Billy
Goat Gruff said to his brothers.
Before they could reply, he clattered
onto the bridge.

At once the troll heard him and raised his massive head. "Who's that trip-trapping across my bridge?" roared the troll.

The littlest Billy Goat stopped short.

"It's only me," he squeaked.

The wicked troll jumped up on the
bridge. He got ready to grab hold
of the littlest Billy Goat.
"I'm going to eat you up," he roared.

"But my brother is much fatter than I am," said the littlest Billy Goat cleverly. "If you are really hungry, you need a good meal."

"Really," said the troll. "You are right. I suppose I could wait for him." So he let the littlest Billy Goat cross his bridge.

Soon the middle-sized Billy Goat
clattered onto the bridge.

"Who's that trip-trapping across my bridge?" the troll roared. He jumped up again and blocked the way across the bridge.

The middle-sized Billy Goat
stopped short.
"It's only me," he said.

"I'm going to eat you up!" roared the wicked troll.

His hands were ready to grab the middle-sized Billy Goat.

"But my brother is even fatter than me," said the middle-sized Billy Goat cleverly. "He would make you a much better

meal than me."

"Really?" said the troll. "You are right. I suppose I could wait for him."
So he let the middle-sized Billy Goat cross his bridge.

Then the biggest Billy Goat left his field
and clattered onto the bridge.

"Who's that trip-trapping across my
bridge?" roared the wicked troll and he
stood in the way of the biggest Billy Goat.

"ME!" bellowed the biggest Billy Goat.

He stamped his hoof.

"I'm going to eat you up," roared the troll, grinning wickedly.

"Oh, no, you're not!" the biggest Billy Goat roared back.

"Oh, yes, I am!" roared the troll, licking his lips.

Then the biggest Billy Goat snorted,

put his head down and charged fiercely.

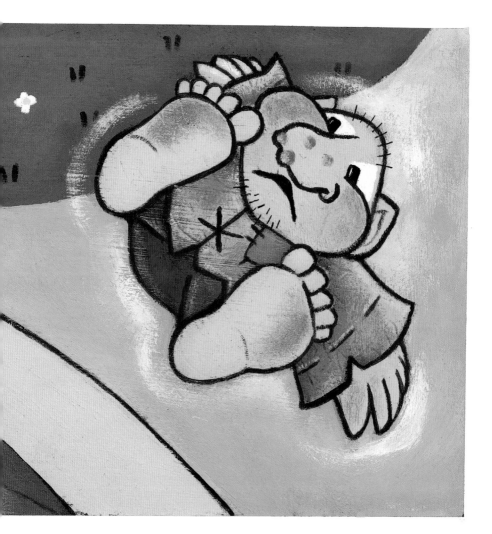

He butted the troll up into the air, right off the bridge and into the river. SPLASH!

The wicked old troll sank under the water and was never seen again.

Now all three Billy Goats had crossed over the bridge. They ate the delicious, sweet grass in the meadow...

...and lived happily ever after.

About the story

The Three Billy Goats Gruff is a fairy tale from Norway. The first version of the story in English appeared in 1859, in a collection by George Webbe Dasent called *Popular Tales from the Norse*. Sometimes the goats appear as grandfather, father and son, but more often they are shown as brothers. There are other stories that have a similar plot of "eat me when I'm fatter". Can you think of another one?

Be in the story!

Imagine you are the troll being interviewed by a newspaper. Describe the Billy Goats Gruff.

Now imagine you are the biggest Billy Goat. Describe the troll and explain why you headbutted him off the bridge.

First published in 2014 by
Franklin Watts
338 Euston Road
London
NW1 3BH

Franklin Watts Australia
Level 17/207 Kent Street
Sydney
NSW 2000

A CIP catalogue record for this book is available
from the British Library.

The artwork for this story first appeared in
Leapfrog: The Three Billy Goats Gruff

ISBN 978 1 4451 2835 1(hbk)
ISBN 978 1 4451 2836 8 (pbk)
ISBN 978 1 4451 2838 2 (library ebook)
ISBN 978 1 4451 2837 5 (ebook)

Series Editor: Jackie Hamley
Series Advisor: Catherine Glavina
Series Designer: Cathryn Gilbert

Printed in China

Franklin Watts is a divison of
Hachette Children's Books,
an Hachette UK company.
www.hachette.co.uk